AF399760

JANE AUSTEN

From humble origins to literary immortality

Written by Julie Pihard
In collaboration with Anne-Sophie Close
Translated by Emma Hanna

Art & Literature   50MINUTES.com

JANE AUSTEN

- **Born:** 16 December 1775 in Steventon.
- **Died:** 18 July 1817 in Winchester.
- **Context:** Romanticism and the Gothic novel are in vogue, tensions between England and France are on the rise and the upheaval of the Industrial Revolution looms on the horizon.
- **Notable works:**
  - *Sense and Sensibility* (1811), novel
  - *Pride and Prejudice* (1813), novel
  - *Mansfield Park* (1814), novel
  - *Emma* (1815), novel
  - *Northanger Abbey* (1817), novel
  - *Persuasion* (1817), novel

At first glance, Jane Austen appears to be no more than a normal, unassuming woman who lived in relative seclusion and favoured a simple, unpretentious literary style. However, appearances can be deceiving, and upon closer inspection her novels reveal an unparalleled gift for description and analysis. Although these talents brought her no recognition during her own lifetime, she has since become one of the most celebrated authors in British literary history.

Her work could be categorised with the sentimental novels which were popular at the time, or it could be a considered a forerunner of realism, which emerged in the following century. However, it is most accurate to say that Austen's style was uniquely her own, and was based solely on her personal observations of humanity. Her refined, elegant novels aimed to paint an accurate, balanced portrait of the domestic environment she had grown up in, namely the world of the landed gentry, and combine an ironic view of the literary trends and current events of the time with extraordinarily insightful descriptions of human emotions, social relations and personal relationships.

Although her novels are unpretentious in style, they brim with charm and wit. In addition to their complex plots, which always reach a satisfying resolution, they feature a wide range of well-developed characters and social commentary, providing plenty of opportunities for humour and even satire. This perfectly balanced combination is the reason why Jane Austen remains one of the most widely read English-language authors not just in the United Kingdom, but throughout the world.

CONTEXT

A PERIOD OF CHANGE AND UPHEAVAL

Jane Austen lived during the reign (1760-1820) of King George III (1738-1820), which was a period of profound changes and widespread turmoil both in Europe and throughout the world.

The transition between the 18th and 19th centuries was a turbulent time in British history, which saw a great deal of political and socio-economic change and heralded even greater change to come. This upheaval began with the loss of Britain's colonies in the Americas, a process which began in 1763 when American citizens rebelled against the taxes levied on them by the British government, which was attempting to replenish the coffers that had been emptied by the Seven Years' War (1756-1763) against France. In 1775, this revolt escalated into the American War of Independence, which only ended when Britain officially recognised the United States of America as an independent country in 1783. The loss of its colonies dealt a heavy blow to the British economy and to the popularity of both the country itself and George III.

In the following years, Britain was embroiled in fresh conflict with France, this time in the form of the Napoleonic Wars (1803-1815), which ended with the defeat of Napoleon Bonaparte (1769-1821) in 1815, but left all of Europe, particularly Britain, in tatters. In 1811, George III's son, the Prince of Wales and the future King George IV (1762-1830), was made regent due to his father's declining mental health, which had left him unfit to rule. Unfortunately, the prince was prone to excess, and racked up enormous debts which emptied the national coffers. However, he was also a loyal patron of the arts, and his regency (1811-1820) and reign (1820-1830) were both characterised by a boom in artistic and intellectual activity. Although Austen held the king in low esteem because of his complacency and lack of self-control, she nevertheless dedicated an edition of her novel *Emma* to him, which was highly appreciated by the monarch.

In addition to the political turmoil which had

arisen as a result of the various wars that had taken place in recent years, poverty was spreading. Taxes and unemployment were constantly rising, and social unrest was becoming more and more common. This period also heralded the start of the Industrial Revolution, which had numerous socio-economic consequences: the rise of new industries, the birth of capitalism, the emergence of the working class, etc. Nevertheless, it is worth pointing out that although Austen uses this period as the backdrop for all of her novels, major political, social and economic events rarely feature in her work. In fact, small towns like the one she lived in remained relatively isolated, and did not undergo the same transformations as larger towns and cities.

THE ORDERED DOMESTIC LIVES OF THE LANDED GENTRY

While Austen rarely mentioned the upheaval that was occurring at that time, she drew a great deal of inspiration from the lives of the English landed gentry in the late 18th century. Their daily routines, their habits and manners, the joys, sorrows, and love they felt and the personal conflicts they faced form the backbone of her stories.

During Austen's time, social hierarchy was rigid and firmly rooted in manners: each individual was expected to behave in a way that was appropriate to their rank and title. More specifically, the members of the landed gentry were well-educated and cultured, and could live comfortably without necessarily being well-off; they were persons of independent means whose income depended on the lands they owned. These individuals were therefore able to indulge in certain leisure pursuits, which were generally determined by their relationships with their peers and their neighbours, with whom they would organise soirees, balls, card tournaments, dinners or hunting expeditions – all of which feature in Austen's novels.

However, her novels are also shaped by the position of women in the society of that era, as was her own life. Women from well-off families were cultured and very well-educated, as this was deemed appropriate for their station, but they were chiefly judged on their level of "accomplishment" and their chances of making a good marriage. Their prospects depended on their beauty, but also on the talents they had and how proficient they were in each one. However, under British law they were not considered to be independent individuals, and therefore had to depend on a man (a father, spouse or brother) to ensure their comfort and financial security throughout their entire lives. They were rarely able to inherit land, as it was almost always left to a brother, cousin or uncle instead, and the careers that were open to them were mostly limited to the roles of governesses and school-teachers. It was therefore almost impossible for a young woman from the landed gentry to claim a legal status and private income of her own at that time. As a writer, which was one of the few activities that were considered suitable for a woman at that time, Austen often explored and questioned the issues of marriage and women's position in society, which are recurring themes throughout all of her novels.

BIOGRAPHY

Portrait of Jane Austen published in *A Memoir of Jane Austen* (1870).

A SLIM BIOGRAPHY

Not much is known about Jane Austen's life. Her existence was quite reclusive and isolated, and most of her limited contact with the outside world was with close relatives. Furthermore, much of her (extensive) correspondence was burned by her sister and confidante Cassandra Elizabeth Austen (1773-1845). Most of the details we know about her were revealed by her brother Henry Thomas Austen (1771-1850), who wrote a biographical preface to a posthumous edition of some of her work, and her nephew, James Edward Austen-Leigh (1798-1874), who wrote *A Memoir of Jane Austen* (1870), a complete biography of his late aunt's life.

Austen was born on 16 December 1775 in the rectory of Steventon, Hampshire. Her father, William George Austen (1731-1805), was a well-off Anglican rector who was part of the landed gentry. He married Cassandra Leigh (1739-1827), a woman of equal social rank, and they had eight children together: James (1765-1819), George (1766-1838), Edward (1767-1852), Henry Thomas, Cassandra Elizabeth, Francis William (1774-1865),

Jane and Charles John (1779-1852). Their sons left home at a young age: James entered the church, Charles and Francis joined the navy, and Henry became a banker (he would later act as Jane's literary agent, and introduced her to some very exclusive London social circles). Meanwhile, Edward was adopted by a cousin, and George, who was mentally disabled, was fostered by another family. The only children who remained at home with their parents were the two girls.

A SOLID EDUCATION

In 1782, Cassandra and Jane Austen were sent to boarding school (in Oxford, Southampton and Reading) to further their education, but they were forced to return home in 1786 because their parents could no longer afford the expense. From that point onwards, their education was mostly overseen by their father, who provided them with an unusually broad, in-depth education for girls of their age and social standing. In particular, he encouraged the young Jane to read a variety of novels from his extensive personal library, which included works by Samuel Richardson (1689-1761), Henry Fielding (1707-1754), Laurence

Sterne (1713-1768) and Walter Scott (1771-1832). These authors would have no small influence on the future author's own literary style and tastes. Austen's upbringing in a cultured home also gave her the chance to participate regularly in plays that were put on by her close relatives, which shaped her love of comedy and satire.

| *The Rice Portrait* (1789), believed to be of Jane Austen and attributed to Ozias Humphry.

She also started writing at a very young age: from 1787 onwards, she appears to have begun keeping notebooks filled with humorous stories, poems and epistolary tales that she wrote to entertain her family, particularly her nieces and nephews. 27 of these early works, which are dated from 1787 to 1793, have been compiled and published under the title *Juvenilia*.

evidence, namely her accurate portrayal of reality, incisive humour, elegant style, etc.

EARLY DRAFTS

Although she always lived the life that was expected of a young woman of her station – she honed her talents (languages, piano, dance, sewing and, of course, reading), helped with the housekeeping, went to church and visited her neighbours – Austen also continued working on increasingly elaborate fictional stories, having evidently made the decision to pursue a career as an author. Between 1793 and 1795, she wrote a short epistolary tale titled *Lady Susan*, and then tried her hand at a prose novel, *Elinor and Marianne*, which served as the first draft for one of her most successful novels, *Sense and Sensibility*. She also fell in love with a man during this time, but they were both aware that marrying was out of the question due to a lack of financial means, and their families soon intervened to keep them apart.

In 1796, Austen began *First Impressions*, an early draft of what would later become *Pride and*

Prejudice. When she submitted it for publication it was refused, and she refocused her attention on editing *Elinor and Marianne* before writing *Susan*, an early draft of *Northanger Abbey*. The manuscript of *Susan* was purchased by a London publisher for a very low price, but was never actually published. In the meantime, the young author began writing *The Watsons*, but it appears that she abandoned her craft for a dozen years or so after that.

In 1801, the family moved to Bath, a town which Austen loathed. Around this time, she accepted a proposal from a local gentleman, but broke off the engagement before they were married. Four years later, her father fell ill and died suddenly, leaving his widow and two unmarried daughters in dire financial straits. The three women then moved to Southampton and only made rare social visits, generally only mixing with other women of equal social station. In 1809, they eventually moved in with Edward, one of the writer's older brothers, in Chawton. This was when Austen began publishing her novels anonymously.

LITERARY SUCCESS

Austen published several books in quick succession: *Sense and Sensibility* in 1811, *Pride and Prejudice* in 1813, *Mansfield Park* in 1814, and *Emma* in 1815. The royalties she earned from these novels were enough for her to make ends meet. Shortly after the publication of *Emma*, she bought the rights to *Susan* back from the original publisher, but she did not publish the novel immediately. She also began working on new projects, notably *Persuasion* (finished in 1816, but only published posthumously in 1817), which is by far the most autobiographical of her novels, and *Northanger Abbey* (1817). In the six months leading up to her death, she began working on her final novel, which was initially titled *The Brothers*, but which was eventually published, unfinished, under the name *Sanditon* (1925).

As she did not have a private study at her disposal, Austen wrote her novels with the hustle and bustle of the household going on around her. She took care to ensure that no one aside from her closest relatives was aware of her writing career. However, this did not hinder her success, as her work nevertheless received praise from renowned authors such as Samuel Taylor Coleridge (1772-1834) and Walter Scott, who published a glowing review of *Emma* in *The Quarterly Review*. However, she did not become a household name until the 1870s, when biographies of her life (including the one written by her nephew) and studies of her work began to appear.

Aside from the few occasions when she moved house and a handful of extended trips away from her home (for example, to London), Austen's life could be described as monotonous, homebound and lacking in ambition; she contented herself with observing the world around her, in which she found an unlimited source of inspiration for her novels.

AN UNTIMELY DEATH

It appears that Austen, who was already suffering from a type of tuberculosis, contracted Addison's disease in 1816 (though it has been argued that her reported symptoms are more consistent with Hodgkin's lymphoma). Although she initially continued to write and publish her novels, she was forced to give up writing in early 1817. Her health was deteriorating rapidly, so she relocated to Winchester with her sister Cassandra and her brother Henry to convalesce. She died there a few months later, on 18 July 1817, and was buried in the city's cathedral.

After the death of their sister, Cassandra and Henry oversaw the joint publication of *Persuasion* and *Northanger Abbey*, which they also used as an opportunity to reveal the author's real name. Since then, Austen's novels have been republished frequently and are famous worldwide. They have also been the subject of many literary and screen adaptations, and neither the general public nor literary critics have ever lost their taste for the work of this humble, middle-class writer from the English countryside, who could probably never have dreamed that her novels would one day occupy such an important position in the global literary canon.

CHARACTERISTICS OF AUSTEN'S WORK

WRITING AGAINST THE GRAIN

The Georgian era was a time when artistic production was flourishing in the disciplines of painting, architecture and literature alike. The writers who were active during this period include great minds like Samuel Johnson (1709-1784), William Wordsworth (1770-1850), John Keats (1795-1821) and Lord Byron (1788-1824). This was also a period when women's educational prospects began to improve in Britain, which accounts for the increase in the number of works of literature that were written by women: among others, these included works by Fanny Burney (1752-1840), Ann Radcliffe (1764-1823), Maria Edgeworth (1767-1849), Mary Shelley (1797-1851) and, of course, Jane Austen.

In the late 18th century, the artistic landscape was dominated by the Romantic and Gothic movements. While Romanticism brought exaggerated sensibility, introspection and universal themes such as death, destiny and evil to the fore, Gothic art and literature relied heavily on clichéd portrayals of horror, the macabre and sentimentalism. However, in the same way that Austen almost entirely disregarded the historical and political context her work was set in, she paid absolutely no attention to the literary trends of the time. Instead of adhering to one of these movements, she mocked and satirised them, preferring to develop an individual style of her own which became her "brand". Her use of irony, her examination of moral issues and her authentic depictions of daily life make her a forerunner of the realist school of literature which became tremendously popular almost a century later. It is also possible to draw comparisons between Austen's work and Symbolism – a reading which suggests that each aspect of her stories (social and familial relationships, significant events, locations, etc.) has a hidden meaning – but literary experts tend to disagree on this subject.

Although her work does not adhere to any particular literary current, some authors do seem to have influenced Austen. It is likely that Burney's novels inspired her focus on women and her feminist themes, while the works of Charlotte Lennox (1730-1804) probably influenced her burlesque humour. Other writers whose work she read and may have been influenced by include Johnson, after whom she may have modelled her calm, biting wit; Fielding, who had a similar passion for parody and satire; and Richardson, to whom Austen makes frequent allusions in her work through her plots, characters who fall into the archetype of the seducer, and the names of her characters and locations.

DOMESTIC THEMES

Austen turned her hand to a wide variety of literary forms, but her major works were all novels. Furthermore, each of her novels features a realistic plot which is generally long and complex, setting her work apart from romances, in which the storylines tend to be more mysterious and feature more imaginary elements.

As well as belonging to the same genre, Austen's works are also all based on her own experiences and personal observations from within her own social class, the landed gentry. In other words, her main goal was to describe what social life was like in the time she lived in. Although her heroines are always from the landed gentry, like she was, Austen also portrays other social classes and the ways they interact. She also takes a keen interest in her protagonists' daily lives, and often provides incredibly specific details about their day-to-day activities, which imbues her work with an unparalleled degree of authenticity. In some ways, her novels are studies of manners, and have often been described as "domestic": Austen observes daily life, no matter how trivial, focusing on a specific location (which is generally limited to three or four families living in the countryside) so that she can provide a nuanced, in-depth analysis of each main character. The extent of the character development in Austen's novels is a testament to her tremendous skill in describing emotions and psychological states.

However, there is a certain degree of tension between the observation of reality and the analysis of emotional impulses in her works. As well as creating a precise, authentic portrayal of the minutiae of everyday life, Austen also commits to a detailed analysis of the characters' interactions, thoughts and misunderstandings, which adds a layer of subjectivity to the text. The heroes – or, as is more often the case, the heroines – are the main subject of this analysis. Austen never relies on clichés or pre-existing archetypes when fleshing out her characters; each of them has their own unique personality and backstory, particularly the young female protagonists, who are usually intelligent and principled. Over the course of each novel, Austen's heroines go through a variety of experiences which allow them to discover their own strengths and weaknesses, becoming more mature as a result. In most cases, this "coming of age" involves their idealistic, romantic illusions being shattered, after which they are brought back to reality, harmony and reason.

Austen also tackles a theme which was particularly close to her heart through her work: the issue of women's position in society, and their dependence on men and marriage. She also subtly incorporates moral themes, such as the subject of how an individual should behave (amiably, sensibly, restrainedly and honourably), as well as addressing more specific, important subjects (particularly the issue of slavery).

AN AUTHENTIC, SIMPLE, SATIRICAL STYLE

The only way to depict reality faithfully is to use an authentic style. As such, Austen's novels are divided into scenes in a manner reminiscent of a play, and they feature a tremendous amount of dialogue in the form of both direct speech and free indirect speech. This narrative style first appeared in English literature in the works of Burney, and is characterised by the absence of an introductory verb denoting speech ("said", "thought", "spoke", "asked", etc.); in other words, it falls somewhere between direct speech and indirect speech. This style gives the story a certain liveliness and fluidity which is highly suited to Austen's goal. It also provides a degree of overlap between the voices of the narrator and the characters, so that the reader is less able to distinguish between them.

Austen generally writes with a light, humorous tone, because she believed that novels should not only educate the reader, but also entertain them. Furthermore, her observation of society was always detached, intelligent, and grounded in restraint: Austen had little fondness for chaotic, exuberant writing styles, and favoured a balanced, measured approach. Her novels are written in a style that is both elegant and precise, balancing rational emotion with a refined sense of detail.

However, all of her works are also flavoured with a certain degree of irony and mischief. Austen had a razor-sharp wit: her social and psychological analyses are highly insightful, and reading between the lines reveals many humorous touches, while her dialogue brims with biting sarcasm. She also does not hesitate to sharply criticise clichés and mediocrity, and often veers into satire. She wrote more than one parody, exaggerating the characteristics of literary styles she found uninspiring as a way of ridiculing them: for example, *Northanger Abbey* is clearly a parody of Radcliffe's Gothic novels, and she mocks epistolary and sentimental novels in one of her earliest efforts, *Love and Freindship*.

NOTABLE WORKS

NORTHANGER ABBEY

The novel which would eventually be published as *Northanger Abbey* was first written in 1797 under the working title *Susan*. Having sold the rights to the novel in 1803 to a publisher who never released the book, Austen bought the rights back in 1816, but it remained unpublished until December 1817, after the author's death, when Henry and Cassandra Austen arranged for it and *Persuasion* to be published as a set. The book was prefaced by a biographical note written by Henry Austen, which remains one of the few reliable sources of information about the author's life that we have access to today. This note was also the first time that Austen was publicly identified as the author of her novels.

Northanger Abbey's plot revolves around the character of Catherine Morland, an innocent, naïve young woman with a great fondness for Gothic novels, particularly those written by Ann Radcliffe, which leads her to get so engrossed in her reading material that she finds it hard to distinguish between fiction and reality. Having fallen in love with a young man named Henry Tilney, she pays a visit to his family home, but begins to suspect his father of terrible crimes and is eventually sent away. Fortunately, Henry realises that something is amiss and straightens the situation out, bringing Catherine back to reality. At the end of the novel she is forgiven and brought back into the fold, and she and Henry get engaged.

Although *Northanger Abbey* was one of the last of Austen's novels to be published, its quality leaves a lot to be desired compared to her other works. Given that the first draft was written very early in her career and did not undergo significant revision, the finished novel does not have Austen's signature depth: the characters are not as well-developed and their emotions and motivations are not analysed as closely as in her other works. Catherine is a virtuous, good-hearted heroine, but her personality is often reduced to her naïveté, making her a somewhat one-dimensional character whose perspective is not quite sufficient to carry the entire novel.

This may be one reason why Austen tends more towards using direct speech than free indirect speech in this novel. However, this stylistic choice is presumably also down to the fact that this book was written when Austen was a much less experienced writer who was still experimenting with different writing styles and had not yet found her own distinctive narrative voice. This lack of maturity also shows in her unbridled criticism of romantic passion and Gothic novels, giving her talent for irony and parody free rein, while melodrama is used both to mock the conventions of Gothic novels and to make the moral of the story more explicit. Austen found the heightened emotions that were portrayed in these novels particularly frustrating, as they clashed with her mild, sensible nature, and therefore adopted a style which was more sarcastic, less subtle, and consequently less balanced than her previously published works.

SENSE AND SENSIBILITY

Austen wrote an early draft of *Sense and Sensibility* in 1797 under the title *Elinor and Marianne.* While the earlier version of the novel was written in epistolary form, Austen rewrote it for publication as a prose novel in 1809, and it was published anonymously in 1811.

The novel focuses on two heroines who are polar opposites: Elinor, an intelligent young woman who is incredibly patient, self-controlled and reserved, and her sister Marianne, a romantic girl whose sensibility often overpowers her common sense. While Elinor keeps her feelings for Edward Ferras a secret, Marianne falls hopelessly in love with John Willoughby, an unscrupulous cad. This means that the two sisters experience their first heartbreak together when they both discover that the man they love is engaged to someone else. Marianne's distress is so great that she falls ill, but she recovers and eventually marries an honest young man who had been trying to win her affections for a long time. Meanwhile, Elinor maintains her composure, and Edward eventually proposes to her after being disinherited and then rejected by his former fiancée, who lost interest in him after he lost his fortune.

| *Marianne in violent affliction*, illustration by Chris Hammond for the 1889 edition of *Sense and Sensibility.*

In addition to the recurring themes of marriage and women's financial dependence on men (as the sisters and their mother are left with no income after the death of their father), the main issue the novel examines is already made evident by the title: which should take precedence, the head (sense) or the heart (sensibility)? The novel has a clear didactic function, as the author uses a logically structured argument to try to show that losing oneself in romantic fancies and sensibility is unhealthy (which is made particularly clear through Marianne's illness), and that it is better to remain grounded. Over the course of the story, Marianne, who is initially portrayed as passionate and lacking in self-control, grows and develops, eventually realising that she will never find happiness unless she listens to good sense. However, although the story is somewhat moralistic, it is still enjoyable thanks to its realistic, well-developed characters, its subtle, elegant style, and its bitingly ironic tone. This is just one example of Austen's balanced approach to writing, and reflects her conviction that literature should not only be instructive, but also entertaining.

Furthermore, Austen uses the character of Marianne to ruthlessly satirise the sentimental novel and Romantic ideologies, offering an almost overt condemnation of the clichés associated with the former (sentimentalism, melodramatic destinies, mysterious characters, fleeting romances, amorous suitors, etc.) and the extremes of the latter (all-consuming passions, idealism, excessive sensibility, turbulent emotions, tormented or dramatic characters, etc.).

PRIDE AND PREJUDICE

Austen started writing *Pride and Prejudice* in 1796 under the title *First Impressions*, but the novel was rejected by a publisher the following year. Following this, she abandoned it for some time, and only rewrote it shortly before it was published in 1813. Like *Sense and Sensibility*, the first edition was published anonymously, and today it is one of the most popular and best-known of all her books.

Mrs Bennet, a rather high-strung woman from Hertfordshire, is determined to marry off her five daughters. Charles Bingley, a rich, attractive young man, has just rented out a neighbouring house and Mrs Bennet soon comes to view him as an excellent match. Although he quickly falls in love with Jane, the eldest of the Bennet sisters, her sisters and his good friend Fitzwilliam Darcy attempt to dissuade him from making the match and keep the two separate. Meanwhile, Mr Darcy is captivated by her younger sister Elizabeth, a spirited young girl with a sharp tongue. He eventually asks her to marry him, but because of the pride he has displayed on previous occasions, she refuses him. He later proves that he has changed by saving her family's reputation, and at the end of the novel Elizabeth agrees to marry him, as does Jane when Bingley comes back to find her and proposes to her.

This is one of Austen's only novels which does not involve the heroine's illusions being shattered, leaving her disappointed; in fact, Elizabeth's spirited nature and ironic wit are somewhat reminiscent of the author herself. Once again, the most important aspects of the novel are not the sequence of events or the overarching plot, but the analysis of the characters' personalities, emotions and relationships. Austen uses satire and irony to focus on the troubles faced by each character, as well as their personal flaws, without allowing the tone to get too serious.

The understated writing style and the realistic depiction of both the characters' emotions and the daily lives of the landed gentry are equally remarkable in this novel. Austen uses subtle touches to describe the lifestyle of the English middle classes towards the end of the 18th century, turning a critical eye on their rituals, customs and habits. The plot chiefly revolves around the themes of marriage and money (once again, an issue related to inheritance has thrown the Bennet sisters' future into jeopardy), and the author condemns the practice of marrying for money, an issue which she addresses from a female perspective which is also decidedly feminist. She also uses the character of Elizabeth to examine the question of whether or not individuals should rebel against the conventions and prejudices the world is built on to form their own opinions.

Given that the novel's plot is chiefly psychological in nature, the characters had to be drawn in exceptional detail to ensure that the story could be resolved satisfactorily. This means that in addition to the four main characters, whose personalities are both highly nuanced and very distinctive, the reader is also introduced to a wide range of secondary characters who are developed in less depth, but still leave a strong impression. In particular, the characters who provide comic relief, such as Mr Collins and Mrs Bennet, are made unforgettable by their simple ways and their exuberance.

EMMA

Emma is one of Austen's later works. She began writing it in 1814, and it was published anonymously in 1815. This book is generally considered Austen's masterpiece, although *Pride and Prejudice* is also a contender for that title.

Emma, a vain, middle-class young woman from a comfortable background, lives alone with her ailing father, Mr Woodhouse. She has certain duties as the lady of the house, but she does not take them very seriously. Instead, she begins shamelessly interfering in the lives of those around her, convinced that her meddling will make their lives happier. In particular, she attempts to arrange a marriage between a less well-off friend of hers, Harriet, and a clergyman, because she believes that the man Harriet has fallen in love with is not good enough for her. However, her pride leads to disaster, and she makes one error of judgement after another. She also falls under the spell of a rakish young man, which ends with her getting her heart broken. She ends up marrying the man whom Harriet had secretly loved all along, while Harriet also marries a suitable man.

| *Emma steering love in the right direction*, illustration by Chris Hammond for the 1898 edition of *Emma*.

This novel was written when Austen was already a mature author, and experts agree that it is a reflection of how well-honed her talents as a novelist had become. Firstly, it is extremely well structured, with a complex, interwoven plot that is reminiscent of detective fiction in certain aspects: clues are scattered throughout the story, the ending is surprising and there is a certain degree of suspense throughout. However, Austen's maturity as a writer is also in evidence in the foundations of the book. Like her other novels, *Emma* is a comedy of manners, and in it, Austen's talent for describing everyday life reaches its apex. The preoccupations, habits and character of the landed gentry of that period are depicted in even greater detail and with even more humour and authenticity than in her previous works, to such an extent that Scott recognised that the novel represented the emergence of a new genre which was based more firmly on realism, and which considered no subject matter beneath its notice. In other words, *Emma* is no less than the forerunner of the genre of realism, which would emerge later in the 19th century.

The incisive emotional analysis in *Emma* is also remarkable. The titular character's personality is incredibly lifelike: her pride and vanity are constantly at odds with her generous spirit and tend to lead her astray while the reader looks on helplessly. The extensive use of free indirect speech also allows the reader to get inside the heroine's head: we discover new information at the same time as her, and feel the same emotions as her, which is one of the book's greatest strengths. But although Austen's intention is to help us to see the world from Emma's perspective, her underlying aim is to allow the reader to learn from the protagonist's mistakes. Just like Emma, we also tend to misinterpret things, judge too quickly or cling so tightly to our pride that we let the chance for happiness pass us by. In this way, the novel aims to make its readers more self-aware.

AUSTEN'S LEGACY

Austen's works were not particularly well-known during most of the 19th century. Although they received a positive reception from a certain literary elite, as well as renowned authors such as Walter Scott, George Eliot (1819-1880) and Henry James (1843-1916), and received favourable attention from some important figures of that period, her novels did not conform to the expectations and trends of the time, as Romanticism was still in vogue. In particular, the Brontë sisters, Charlotte (1816-1855), Emily (1818-1848) and Anne (1820-1849), were extremely critical of Austen's novels due to their lack of passion and their measured tone.

However, when her nephew published *A Memoir of Jane Austen* a few decades later, interest in the author's work surged and she became a household name. By the 20th century, her novels were being widely studied and analysed, and Austen had been ushered into the ranks of the best-loved writers in the history of English-language literature. Today, she remains one of the most popular and most frequently translated English-language authors in the world, and her fans are so fervent in their admiration for their work that they even have their own name: the "Janeites".

As a pioneer of the domestic novel and a forerunner of the realist current that would emerge later in the 19th century, Austen's work was an inspiration for venerated authors such as Thomas Love Peacock (1785-1866), Charles Dickens (1812-1870), Rudyard Kipling (1865-1936) and Virginia Woolf (1882-1941). Her novels have also been the subject of many literary adaptations, continuations and homages, such as *Bridget Jones's Diary* (1996) by Helen Fielding (born in 1958) and *Death Comes to Pemberley* (2011) by P. D. James (1920-2014). However, the influence of Austen's work has also extended beyond the literary sphere in more recent decades, and her novels have been the subject of numerous adaptations for both television and cinema. Notable examples include the 1995 television miniseries *Pride and Prejudice* by director Simon Langton (born in 1941) and the film *Mansfield Park* (1983) by David Giles (1926-

2010). In fact, all of Austen's novels have been the subject of at least one adaptation, including *Pride and Prejudice* (2005) by Joe Wright (born in 1972), *Emma* (1996) by Douglas McGrath (born in 1958) and *Sense and Sensibility* (1995) by Ang Lee (born in 1954). Finally, the life of the writer herself has inspired many works of literature and film, notably the recent film *Becoming Jane* (2007), a loose biography directed by Julian Jarrold (born in 1960).

In just two centuries, Jane Austen's legacy has been transformed from that of a humble, country-dwelling writer to that of one of the best-known figures in literary history. Today, she remains as beloved as ever by her flocks of adoring Janeites, who show no signs of flagging in their devotion or allowing her to be forgotten any time soon.

SUMMARY

- Jane Austen was a humble, unassuming woman who never sought the fame and recognition she gained after her death. In fact, most of her novels were originally published anonymously. She was a lifelong spinster who lost her father at a relatively young age and who lived a quiet, uneventful life surrounded by her closest relatives.
- As her knowledge of the outside world was fairly limited, she found inspiration in the world of the landed gentry she was raised in, and mastered the art of observing and analysing human relationships and emotions.
- Her works are realistic and authentic, which is generally seen as one of her greatest strengths as a writer, and her elegant, understated writing style is exceedingly balanced (particularly in the novels written later in her career). She has a particular fondness for free indirect speech, which she uses to blur the lines between the third-person narrator and her heroines, which allows readers to immerse themselves more

fully in the characters' thoughts and feelings.

- Most of her novels were chiefly instructive in nature: Austen favoured reason over emotion, and used her novels to try to demonstrate to her readers that excessive passion does not lead to happiness any more than denying one's emotions does.
- However, her novels were written to be entertaining as well as educational, and often feature biting wit, irony and even satire.
- Although critics generally ignored Austen's work until the last few decades of the 19th century, this was because she was ahead of her time: in addition to being a pioneer of the domestic novel and literary realism, she also questioned the way society marginalised women during that era. However, her talent was finally recognised in the 20th century, and today her works are among the most frequently read, translated and adapted novels in the world, making her one of the most influential writers in the English language.

We want to hear from you!
Leave a comment on your online library
and share your favourite books on social media!

FURTHER READING

BIBLIOGRAPHY

- Albert, E. (1979) *History of English Literature.* London: Harrap.

- Austen, J. (2000) *Emma.* Ware: Wordsworth.

- Austen, J. (1993) *Persuasion.* Ware: Wordsworth.

- Austen, J. (1992) *Northanger Abbey.* Ware: Wordsworth.

- Austen, J. (1992) *Pride and Prejudice.* Ware: Wordsworth.

- Austen, J. (1992) *Sense and Sensibility.* Ware: Wordsworth.

- Beer, G. (1981) Les Victoriennes. *Magazine littéraire.* 177, pp. 13-17.

- Browning, D. C. ed. (1969) *Dictionary of Literary Biography. English and American.* London/New York: J.-M. Dent & Sons/E.P. Dutton & Co.

- Cecil, D. (2000) *A Portrait of Jane Austen.* London: Penguin.

- Clarac, P. ed. (1961) *Dictionnaire universel des lettres.* Paris: Société d'édition de dictionnaires et encyclopédies.

- (2003) *Encyclopédie de la littérature*. Paris: Librairie générale française.

- Coustillas, P., Petit, J.-P. and Raimond, J. (1978) *Le Roman anglais au xixe siècle*. Paris: PUF.

- Drabble, M. and Stringer, J. eds. (2007) *The Concise Oxford Companion to English Literature*. Oxford: Oxford University Press.

- Eagle, D. (1970) *The Concise Oxford Dictionary of English Literature*. Oxford: Oxford University Press.

- Ford, B. ed. (1982) From Blake to Byron. *The New Pelican Guide to English Literature*. Vol. 5. Harmonsworth: Penguin.

- Gillie, C. (1974) *A Preface to Jane Austen*. London: Longman.

- Hardy, B. (1975) *A Reading of Jane Austen*. London: Peter Owen.

- Harvay, P. ed. (1967) *The Oxford Companion to English Literature*. Oxford: Clarendon Press.

- Jack, I. (1963) *English Literature: 1815-1832*. Oxford: Clarendon Press.

- Laffont, R. and Bompiani, V. eds. (1994) *Le Nouveau Dictionnaire des œuvres de tous les temps et de tous les pays*. Vols. 1, 2, 4 and 5. Paris: Laffont.

- Le Faye, D. (2003) *Jane Austen: the World of Her Novels*. London: Frances Lincoln.

- Minois, G. (1998) *L'Angleterre géorgienne*. Paris:

PUF.

- Pinion, F. B. (1973) *A Jane Austen Companion.* London/Basingstoke: MacMillan Press.

- Pirie, D. ed. (1994) *The Romantic Period.* London: Penguin.

- Richardson, A. E. (2008) *Georgian England.* Lindley: Jeremy Mills Publishing.

- Stokes, M. (1991) *The Language of Jane Austen.* Houndmills/London: MacMillan.

- Teyssandier, H. (1977) *Les Formes de la création Romanesque à l'époque de Walter Scott et de Jane Austen (1814-1820).* Paris: Didier.

- Todd, J. M. (2005) *Jane Austen in Context.* Cambridge: Cambridge University Press.

- Van Tieghem, P. ed. (1968) *Dictionnaire des littératures.* Vol. 1. Paris: PUF. 1968.

- Wright, A. H. (1972) *Jane Austen's Novels: A Study in Structure.* Harmondsworth: Penguin.

ADDITIONAL SOURCES

- *The Real Jane Austen.* (2002) [Television film]. Nicky Pattison. Dir. UK: BBC.

- *Jane Austen Centre* website: <http://www.janeausten.co.uk>

- *Jane Austen Society* website: <http://www.janeaustensoci.freeuk.com>

- Visits to Jane Austen's house: <http://www.jane-austens-house-museum.org.uk>

ICONOGRAPHIC SOURCES

- Portrait of Jane Austen published in *A Memoir of Jane Austen* (1870). Royalty-free reproduction picture.

- *The Rice Portrait* (1789), believed to be of Jane Austen and attributed to Ozias Humphry. Royalty-free reproduction picture.

- *Marianne in violent affliction*, illustration by Chris Hammond for the 1889 edition of *Sense and Sensibility*. Royalty-free reproduction picture.

- *Emma steering love in the right direction*, illustration by Chris Hammond for the 1898 edition of *Emma*. Royalty-free reproduction picture.

www.50minutes.com

Ebook EAN: 9782808005128

Paperback EAN: 9782808005135

Legal Deposit: D/2017/12603/794

Cover: © Primento

Digital conception by Primento, the digital partner of publishers.